BECOME A BIRD
AND FLY!

BECOME A BIRD AND

FLY!

MICHAEL ELSOHN ROSS

ILLUSTRATED BY PETER PARNALL

THE MILLBROOK PRESS
BROOKFIELD, CONNECTICUT

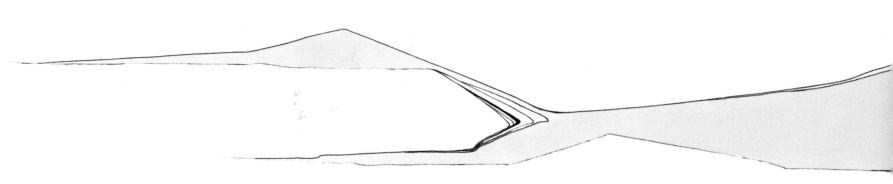

Library of Congress Cataloging-in-Publication Data

Ross, Michael Elsohn, 1952–
Become a bird and fly! / by Michael Elsohn Ross ; illustrated by Peter Parnall.
    p.   cm.
Summary: Using his imagination, Nicky changes into a bird and takes flight.
ISBN 1-56294-074-0 (LIB.)
[1. Birds—Fiction. 2. Flight—Fiction. 3. Imagination–Fiction.]
I. Parnall, Peter, ill. II. Title.
PZ7.R719725Be 1992
[E]—dc20   91-36562 CIP AC

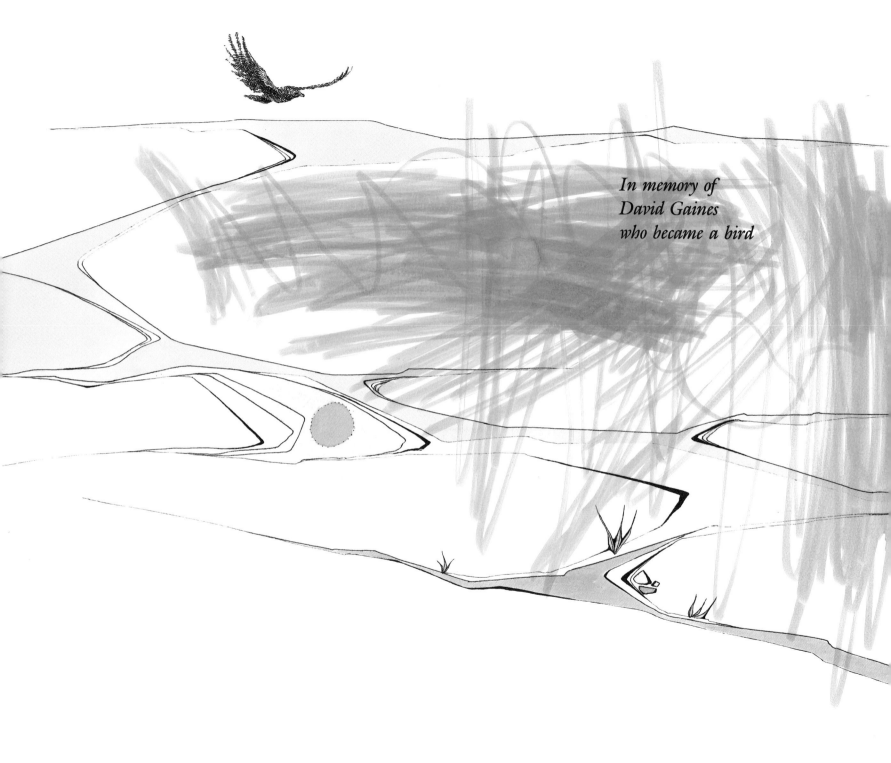

In memory of
David Gaines
who became a bird

Nicky loved to watch birds fly.
Sometimes he tried to fly too.
He flapped and fluttered and flailed.
He ran and jumped and dived.

But still, he couldn't fly like birds.

Nicky's neighbor, Avis, often watched him from her garden.
One day she called out to him,
  "Hey, come here, you bird pretender!
  Would you really like to take off and fly high in the sky?"

  "Yes, oh yes!" he replied.

Avis stared deep into Nicky's eyes and spoke softly,
  "Your mind is like the sky—
  It is wide and full and infinitely high.
  Close your eyes . . . let your thoughts take wing.

Think about becoming a bird.

"Birds are not heavy, so imagine that you are growing lighter.
Your hair falls off and your fat disappears.
Your clothes are now a layer of warm, airy feathers.

"A bird is streamlined.
  Feel your head grow sleek.
  Those are feathers growing on your rear.
  Why? As you fly, they'll help you glide and steer . . .

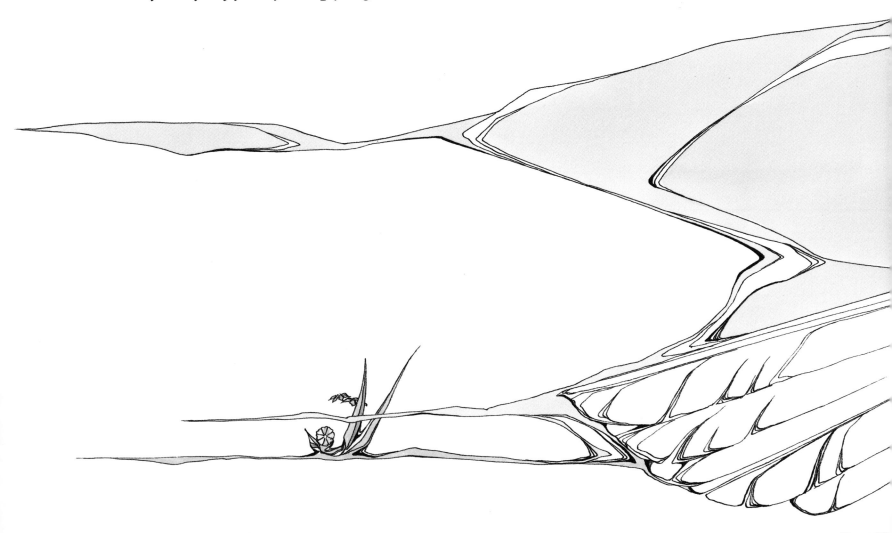

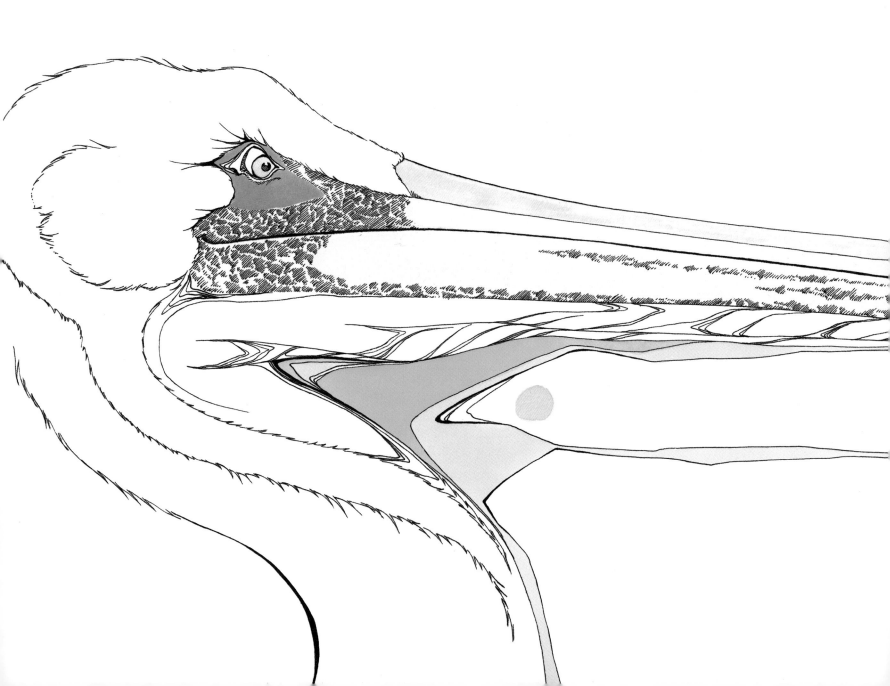

"You become lighter still as your bones fill with air.
Your heavy teeth fall out.
Your jaws turn into a beak.

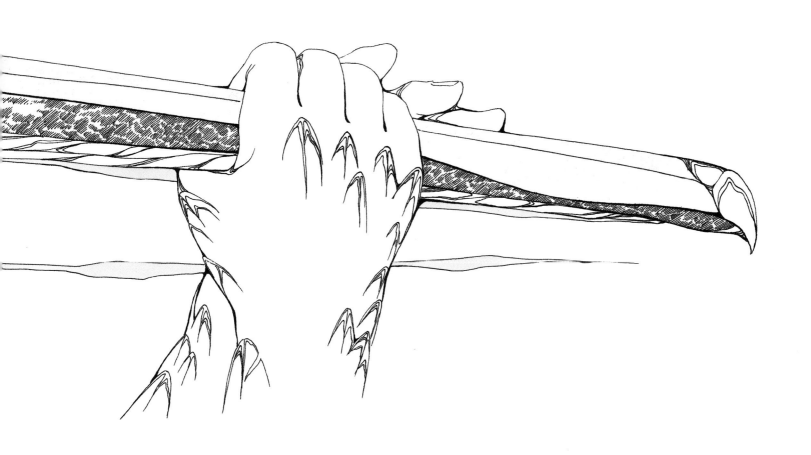

"*A bird needs wings to swim in the air.*
Stretch out your arms and spread your fingers.
Feel long feathers unfold.
Feel the air whoosh as you flap . . .
and flap . . .

and flap.

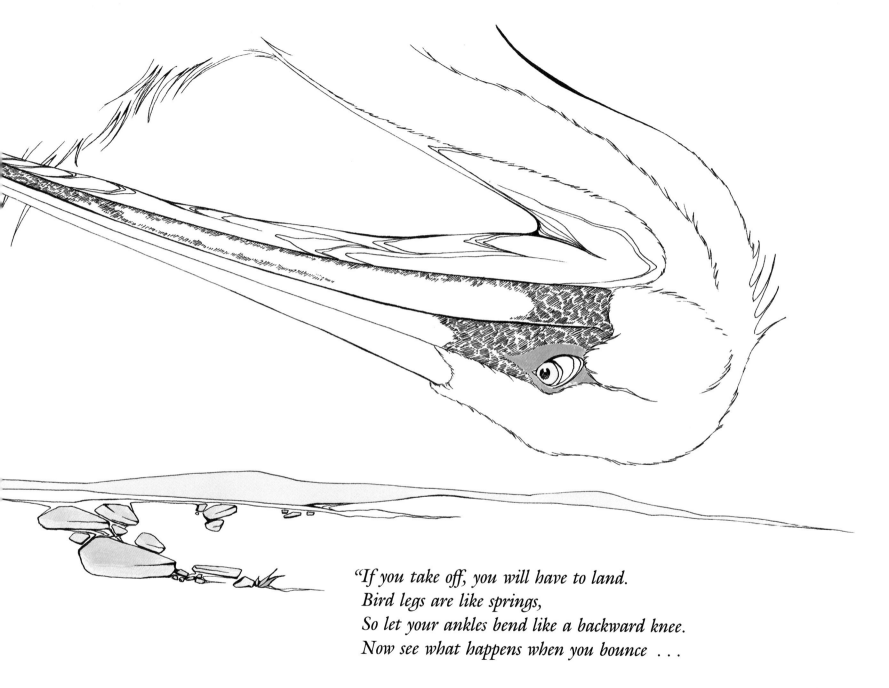

*"If you take off, you will have to land.
Bird legs are like springs,
So let your ankles bend like a backward knee.
Now see what happens when you bounce . . .*

"You feel like a bird now.
 Your heart beats fast.
 Your wings ache.
 Your stomach complains.
 You need strong muscles and food . . . lots of food.
 All day long you need food.

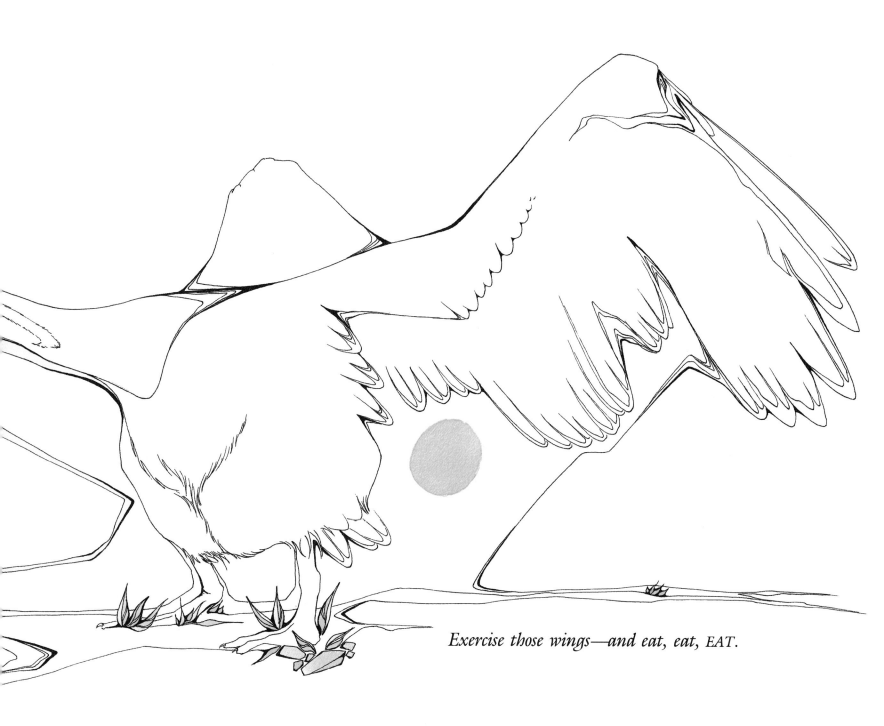

Exercise those wings—and eat, eat, EAT.

"The time has come to go into the sky.
Try and try and try . . .

Now flap your wings

And . . . fly!"

Nicky rose into the sky.

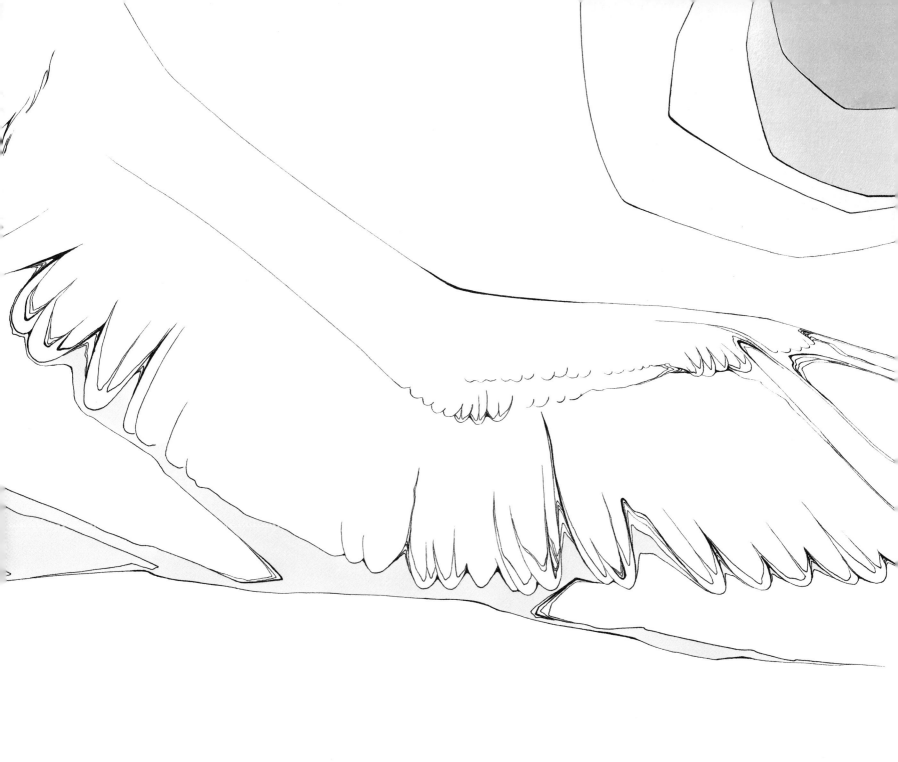

He swooped.

He dived.

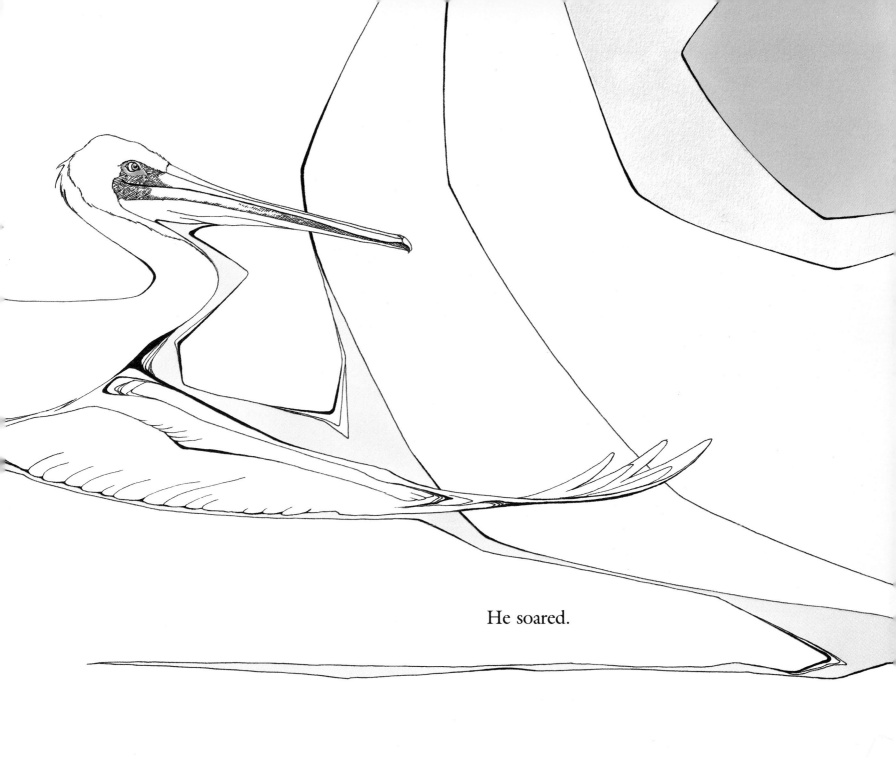

He soared.

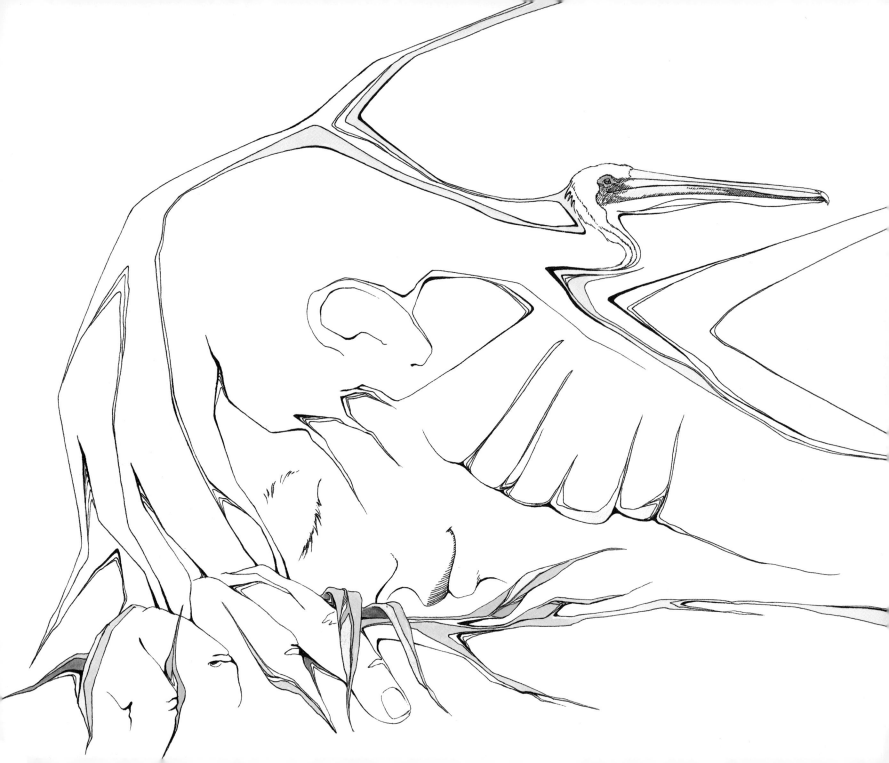

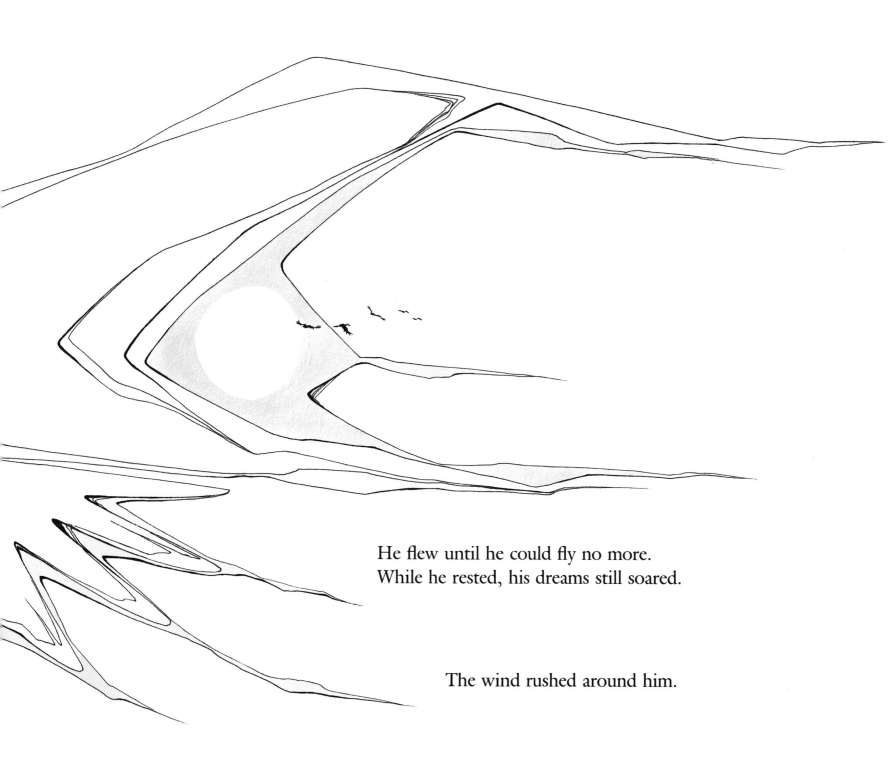

He flew until he could fly no more.
While he rested, his dreams still soared.

The wind rushed around him.

Nicky awoke . . . he was a boy again.
But in his hand . . .

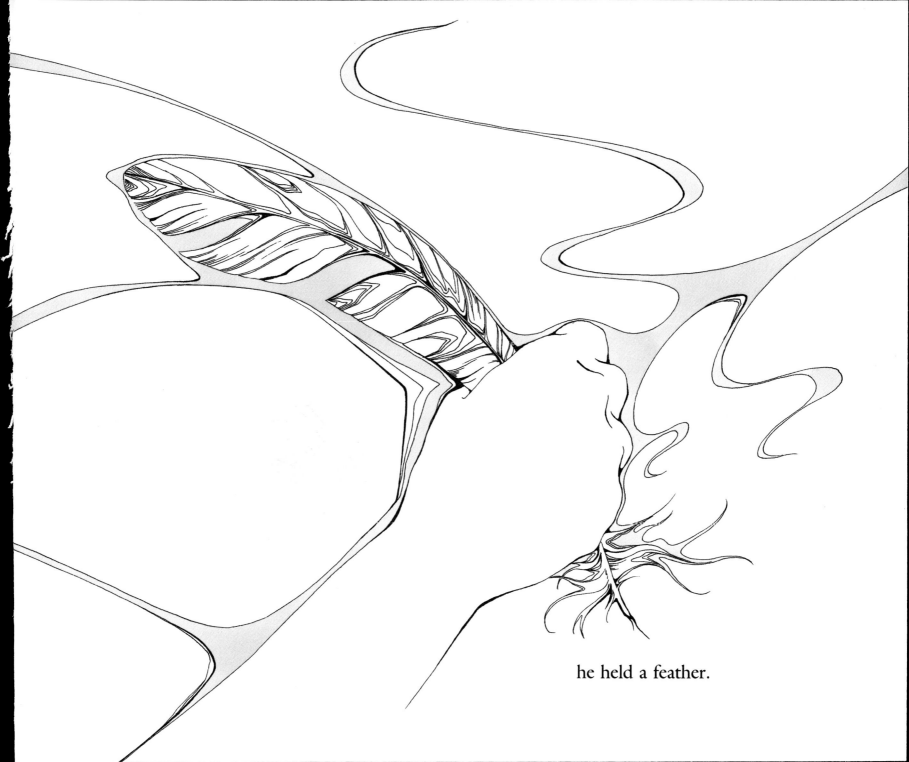

he held a feather.

About the Author

When the author was a small boy in Huntington, New York, he watched in awe as another boy jumped off a garage roof, flapped his arms and tried to fly. The would-be flyer didn't get very far — in fact he broke his arm — but Michael understood exactly why he jumped. Later, as a young man, Michael Elsohn Ross went to Yosemite National Park to work as a naturalist. Birds were everywhere. Sometimes when he took people on a bird-seeking expedition, he would lead them to a high perch where they could look down on the meadows and forests. He would ask them to close their eyes while he helped them imagine changing into birds. This book came from those dreams of flying.

Trained in early-childhood education and conservation, Michael Ross develops primary grade science activities and presents teaching workshops. He has also worked as an entomologist on biological control research projects. He is the author and illustrator of many books for young people, among them *What Makes Everything Go? An Energy Primer, Faces in All Kinds of Places,* and *The Yosemite Fun Book: A Kid's Guide to Yosemite.*

About the Artist

Peter Parnall, too, has been a life-long student of animal behavior, the out-of-doors, and nature in general — interests that are reflected in the more than eighty books he has illustrated. Three of these books have been named Caldecott Honor Books and several have been on the *New York Times* "Best Illustrated Books of the Year" list. His artwork has been exhibited in numerous fine-art museums and he has had over three dozen one-artist shows.

An author as well as an artist, he has written and illustrated a number of books for young people, including *Cats from Away, Winterbarn, Woodpile, The Rock,* and *Marshcat. The Daywatchers,* an illustrated collection of stories about his personal relationships with hawks and eagles, won the New York Academy of Sciences' Children's Book Award.

From his farm on the Maine coast, Peter Parnall pursues a number of interests, among them training horses, woodland management, and caring for the inhabitants of a bonsai nursery.

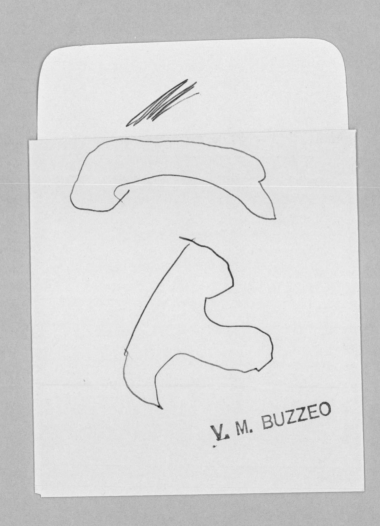

V. M. BUZZEO